FREE WILLY 3
THE RESCUE

Adapted by Nancy Krulik
Based on the screenplay written by John Mattson
and characters created by Keith A. Walker

© 1997 Warner Bros.

SCHOLASTIC INC.

New York Toronto London Auckland Sydney

ISBN 0-590-37405-2

12 11 10 9 8 7 6 5 4 3 2 1   7 8 9/9 0 1 2/0

Designed by Joan Ferrigno

Printed in the U.S.A.

First Scholastic printing, August 1997

"The orca population has been shrinking in the past two years, and we don't know why."

Jesse listened carefully as Drew, a marine biologist, spoke to the captain and crew of the *Noah*. They were about to set sail on a very important mission.

It was a mission that could save thousands of whales' lives.

Jesse was very proud to be part of the crew of the *Noah*. He would be helping his friend Randolph and Drew tag pods of orca with electronic devices. The tags would allow them to track the whales anywhere on the planet, twenty-four hours a day. Hopefully they would be able to discover just what was causing all the deaths.

Jesse was worried about all the orcas. But he was especially concerned about one—his old friend, Willy.

There was only one sure way to find out if Willy was okay. Jesse would have to call him.

Jesse had first met Willy years ago at an amusement park. Willy was a prisoner in the park, and Jesse was the one who freed him. Back then, the two communicated through music. Jesse would blow a tune on his harmonica. When Willy heard the song, he would come running.

Now Willy swam free in the ocean. Surely he was too far away from the *Noah* to hear an ordinary harmonica. So Jesse recorded the song and played it loudly through the ocean with a special microphone. If Willy was anywhere within thirty miles of the *Noah*, he would hear the song—and come to Jesse.

One night, while Jesse was sleeping, he felt something collide with the *Noah*. The boy went up on deck and saw a beautiful orca with three spots on his side. *Willy!*

The whale let out a mournful cry. *Something was terribly wrong.*

When Randolph and Drew heard Willy's cry, they also ran up on deck.
    "Something's happened," Jesse told them. Jesse and Randolph quickly climbed into the *Noah*'s small rubber dinghy. They motored toward Willy. That's when Jesse spotted a sharp spear sticking in Willy's tail!
    "There are whalers here, Randolph," Jesse whispered nervously.
    Randolph leaned over and tried to remove the spear. But the killer whale thrashed his tail wildly. Willy wouldn't let anyone near him.
    "We have to get that spear out before infection sets in," Randolph insisted. "We'll try again tomorrow."

Willy let out a loud, sad cry.

"What's he doing?" Drew asked as Jesse got back aboard the *Noah*.

"He's calling his family," Jesse explained.

By the next morning, the members of Willy's pod were all swimming around the *Noah*. Willy seemed calmer.

Jesse, Drew, and Randolph got in the dinghy. Jesse put on his scuba gear and swam underneath Willy's tail. He used cable cutters to clip the end of the spear and quickly pulled the rest of it out. He watched curiously as Willy playfully bumped noses with a beautiful female orca. "Who's that with Willy?" Jesse asked Randolph.

"That's Nicky," Randolph replied. "I spent some time with her back in Puget Sound. We're old friends."

Nicky swam up to the boat; Willy followed closely behind. Randolph reached over and placed an electronic tag on Willy's fin.

As Randolph tagged Nicky, he noticed something different about her. He pulled out a heart monitor and placed it on the whale's head. Then he smiled broadly.

Drew listened to the monitor. "Either Nicky has two hearts, or she's going to have a baby," she told Jesse.

Willy was going to be a father!

Just then a huge fishing boat appeared on the horizon. It seemed harmless enough to Randolph and Jesse.

But Willy knew that it was no harmless ship. It was a whaling ship. The people on the boat had killed members of his pod, and tried to kill him. Willy raced angrily through the water and splashed at the boat with his tail.

"It's them!" Jesse cried out. "They're the ones who put the spear in Willy. Willy wouldn't do that if it wasn't them!"

Jesse wanted the captain of the *Noah* to report the fishing boat to the authorities. But the captain refused.

"There's nothing to call in," he said. "That boat is the *Botany Bay*, a registered salmon boat. Its captain's record is clean. You have no proof of whaling."

Proof. If that's what the captain needed, Jesse would get it for him. But that would take time. Willy needed protection *now*.

Quickly, Jesse activated his computer. The harmonica sounds floated out through the water. As long as the song played, Willy would stay near. And if he stayed near, he would be safe. Hopefully . . .

Once he was sure that Willy and the rest of his pod were safe, Jesse set off to check out the *Botany Bay*. He knew the boat's crew were not harmless salmon fishermen. He just had to find a way to prove it to the captain.

Jesse watched as the crew of the *Botany Bay* left the boat and went into town. Now was his chance!

Jesse grew nervous as he approached the *Botany Bay*. This could be dangerous. But Jesse knew he couldn't turn back now. Willy needed him.

Slowly, Jesse climbed onboard. He looked around. No one was there. He walked quietly around the corner . . .

"What do you want?" a voice shouted out at him.

Jesse jumped. He had no idea anyone was aboard. He looked down to see a small boy, about ten years old.

"I'm looking for work as a fisherman," Jesse lied.

Just then Jesse felt a heavy hand land squarely on his shoulder. He looked up into the cold brown eyes of the *Botany Bay*'s captain.

"Max, why don't you show your friend out," the captain ordered his son.

"He's not my friend, Dad," the boy insisted as he led Jesse off the deck of the *Botany Bay*.

Jesse followed Max to the town library. Max went to the shelves and pulled out all sorts of books about whaling. Jesse watched the boy grimace as picture after picture of whales being killed passed before his eyes. Obviously, Max didn't like what his father did for a living.

"What your dad is doing is wrong, Max," Jesse said quietly, taking a seat beside Max.

"Why do you care anyway?" Max asked. But behind Max's tough attitude, Jesse could tell Max knew whaling was wrong.

"Your dad is hurting my friends, Max," Jesse said simply.

Friends that are whales? Max found that one hard to believe. "I'll bet you haven't even seen a whale," he said.

Jesse just smiled. "You want to meet some?" he asked.

Jesse brought Max back to the *Noah*. Then, using the tracking device, he was able to locate Willy and the pod right away.

Jesse and Max hopped into the *Noah*'s small dinghy and motored out toward the pod.

"Listen," Jesse whispered to Max. "They're close."
Max tilted his head slightly. He could hear the whales singing.
"It's quite a sound, isn't it?" Jesse asked him. "When a whale sings you can feel the beat of his song in time with the waves."
Suddenly the small boat lurched forward. Max gasped. But Jesse laughed. It was just Willy playing a game.

"Hey, boy!" Jesse greeted Willy.
Willy showered the boys with water from his blowhole. Then he disappeared under the water.
"He likes to play games," Jesse told Max. "Fetch is his favorite."
"What does he fetch?" Max asked.
"Just follow me," Jesse said as he climbed into the water.

It didn't take long for Max to realize that Willy was fetching him! Willy swam right up to Max and put his face in the boy's stomach. *Whish!* Max soared into the air!

"I've never seen him take to any one like that before," Jesse told Max. "He's only like that with family."

Max smiled. He felt like Willy was family, too. He decided he would do whatever it took to keep him safe.

That night, when the crew of the *Botany Bay* went into town for a hot meal, Jesse snuck onboard. He found a small hatch in the deck. Quietly he opened the door and went below.

Jesse found what he was looking for. He saw a spear like the one in Willy's tail and some other whaling spears.

"I think I've hit the jackpot," Jesse whispered.

Jesse grabbed one of the spears and began to climb back on deck. But before he could open the hatch, Jesse heard voices.

"Let's get back out to sea," one man said.

Jesse recognized that voice. It was Max's father, the captain of the *Botany Bay*.

"Yes, sir," a man with a deep voice answered.

As the men walked away, Jesse scurried back on deck. But before he could reach the edge of the boat, the spear slipped from his grip and landed with a loud clang on the deck.

Before Jesse knew it, the *Botany Bay* was pulling away from the dock. If he didn't get out of there soon he'd be stuck at sea with a crew of vicious whalers!

But Jesse couldn't leave without the spear. It was the proof he needed to stop the *Botany Bay* from killing Willy and his family.

Suddenly, someone snuck up behind Jesse and tapped him on the back. Jesse spun around, startled.

"You dropped this," Max said as he handed Jesse the spear. Jesse took the spear from his hand and looked over the rail. The ship was getting farther and farther from the dock.

"What are we going to do?" Max asked Jesse.

"We're going to get the coastal marine patrol. But we're going to have to swim to shore."

Max shook his head. "*We* are not," he declared. "I can't swim that far. I'll stay here and do what I can to help."

Jesse nodded. Then, holding the spear tightly in his hand, he dove off the side of the boat and swam away into the dark night.

The second Jesse hit the shore, he raced into town. There was no time to waste in trying to stop the whalers on the *Botany Bay*.

Jesse found the captain of the *Noah* sitting in a restaurant with Randolph and Drew. He raced over to the table and shoved the spear right under the captain's nose.

"There's your proof," Jesse declared. "This is the same kind of spear we pulled out of Willy. It's a spear that was below the deck of the *Botany Bay*."

The captain nodded. "We'll call it in first thing in the morning," he said.

Jesse shook his head. "They have a head start," he cried out. "They're already back at sea. We can catch them red-handed."

But the captain stood his ground. He wasn't doing anything until the morning. But Willy might not be able to wait until morning.

Jesse shrugged and left the restaurant. It was time for Plan B.

22

Randolph met up with Jesse aboard the *Noah*. Jesse told him about Plan B. While everyone was still in town, Jesse wanted to steal the *Noah* and sail off to save Willy.

Randolph was worried. "Piracy is what they call that!" he exclaimed. "Ten years in jail. Do not pass go. Do not collect two hundred dollars!"

But Jesse was determined. And Randolph agreed to help him. After all, he couldn't let the kid go out there all by himself.

Randolph snuck into the first mate's cabin to look for the spare key. Drew heard noises coming from the cabin. When she discovered Randolph, she was not happy.

"You're stealing the boat and going after the whalers?" she asked nervously.

Randolph nodded slowly.

"You'll go to jail," she declared. "Why are you doing this?"

"Because it's the right thing to do," Randolph said quietly.

Drew couldn't argue with that. In fact, she wanted to help. The three of them set off after the *Botany Bay*.

   Before long Jesse spotted Willy's pod through his
binoculars. He also saw the *Botany Bay*. It was heading toward the
whales. Max wanted to help Willy, but he was locked up in the ship's
cabin.

   Jesse hoped the whales would swim away to safety. But instead of
turning away, the pod of whales swam straight for the *Botany Bay*!

   Jesse dropped everything and raced to his computer. He watched
as sound waves flashed across the screen. The *Botany Bay* had stolen
Willy's song! They'd recorded it and broadcast it out into the sea. The
very song Jesse had recorded to help keep Willy safe was now placing
him in grave danger.

"Willy won't know the difference," he cried out. "They're swimming into a trap!"

Jesse watched, terrified, through his binoculars. He saw Max appear on board. And then the strangest thing happened. The *Botany Bay* turned *away* from the whales.

"Why would they do that?" Randolph questioned.

Jesse watched as the captain of the *Botany Bay* lowered himself on a ladder toward the water. He stuck his hand out and tossed a life ring to a young boy.

Max had jumped overboard!

Jesse smiled. The kid had found a way to stop the *Botany Bay* and help Willy.

But Jesse's joy was short-lived. The *Botany Bay* was soon back on course. The captain and his crew were determined to kill those whales!

Jesse had to think fast. He raced over to the ship's radio and called the coastal marine patrol.

"This is the *Noah*. There's been a collision! SOS," Jesse shouted. He hoped the coastal marine patrol would rush to the scene—and arrive in time to stop the whalers on the *Botany Bay*.

CRASH!

Just then, the *Botany Bay* was hit with a force so strong, it knocked the harpoon right from its captain's hands. But the ship wasn't hit by a whale. It was hit by the *Noah*. Jesse ran the ship into the *Botany Bay*.

The force of the collision sent the crew of the *Botany Bay* careening backward. The captain was thrown overboard. Instantly, Willy swam to the captain.

Now the whaling captain was face-to-face with his former prey.

Suddenly, the mast that held the whaling net collapsed! The net fell into the water below, catching the captain in its threads. The captain thrashed wildly, trying to free himself from the trap.

Willy's big brown eyes peered into the captain's. It was as though he was asking, How do *you* like it?

Willy pressed his snout firmly against the captain's back . . . and pushed him safely to the surface.

The marine coastal patrol arrived and boarded the *Botany Bay*. The crew's whaling days were over. Jesse, Randolph, and Drew watched as the captain hugged his son. Jesse grinned. Max and Willy had finally gotten their message across.

"It's not what I would have done," Drew remarked as Willy's pod swam off safely. "A guy tries to kill me, I wouldn't have saved him. I would have eaten him."

"Maybe Willy's just smarter than we are," Jesse responded.

"Or more human," Randolph suggested.

A few days later, Jesse, Max, Drew, and Randolph watched as Willy and Nicky swam peacefully in the cool blue water. Suddenly Nicky broke away from Willy. She turned slowly on her side and with one powerful push, forced a baby whale into the water.

The baby whale had three spots, just like his father. Jesse gave him the perfect name . . .

Max!